The Moon Has A Tune

Written and Illustrated by
Laura E. Lemon

Balboa Press books may be ordered through booksellers or by contacting:

Balboa Press
A Division of Hay House
1663 Liberty Drive
Bloomington, IN 47403
www.balboapress.com
1 (877) 407-4847

Interior Image Credit: Laura E. Lemon

ISBN: 978-1-9822-4661-7 (sc)
ISBN: 978-1-9822-4777-5 (hc)
ISBN: 978-1-9822-4660-0 (e)

Library of Congress Control Number: 2020907044

Print information available on the last page.

Balboa Press rev. date: 05/12/2020

BALBOA.PRESS
A DIVISION OF HAY HOUSE

To our children. Magical moments for young and old alike.

The Moon Has A Tune

There once was a girl who lay in a bed.
Her blankets were snuggled up, close to her head.
She drifted through dreams, beneath the bright moon.
'Till something awoke her. A magical tune.

The song became louder. Now closer, it grew.
The lyrics so eerie...like shades of dark blue.
It floated through trees, the wind and the air.
Through lifted soft breeze. Who sang it? From where?

It called her to wake. 'It's time to arise.
Come see the bright moon. Just open your eyes.
The day is beginning. The world is anew.
See what lies ahead. What dreams may come true?'

She threw back the covers and rose from her bed.
She stretched and she reached up over her head.
Then outside the window, what once was so near,
The song began fading, or so it appeared.

She fetched her wool sweater, her hat and her boots,
And snuck down the stairs in silent pursuit.
So careful she stepped, upon tippy toe.
'Try hard not to wake them for no one must know.'

She fled through the grass,
it sparkled with dew.
Bright frigid wet crystals.
The day was so new.
The song became clearer. The air felt so still.
The dawn slowly broke through
morning's cold chill.

She then saw a figure, a dark silhouette.
It scraped at the ground.
Bent low as it crept.
It searched for small pieces,
Or parts of a tree.
Put things in a bag, what
could those things be?

The girl's mind did wonder. She
questioned just who?
Who is this dark person? A
crooked old shrew?
A witch or a crone? Just who could it be?
She hobbles along with stiff bended knee.

And then the witch turned.
So slowly she looked.
She peered towards the girl.
Her hands how they shook.
Then as the witch stood and
opened her mouth,
A silence crept over the
trees from the south.

And as the witch swayed, she
smiled and she sang,
The sweet melody. It mystically rang.
Her voice pure and sweet, so
bright and so clear.
How could it belong to this
old hag she feared?

The crone again bent, slow
down to the ground,
And lifted a ball, rough ugly and round.
She put the round thing right into a bag.
A bag that befits a ragged old hag.

The girl thought, 'Just RUN,
it's time to now go.'
Then something crept softly
across her big toe.
A cat! How it purred. It twisted its tail.
It snuggled up close. Its
comfort prevailed.

'It's soft and it's warm, but
black as the night,'
The girl thought while looking
upon the cat's sight.
"What have you got there?"
The old witch she said.
Now standing up over,
above the girl's head.

"My cat? How she likes you.
I clearly can see,
How special you are. You must follow me."
The girl looked not knowing.
Just what she should do?
With courage she rose to
face the old shrew.

And just as she stood, she
saw with surprise,
The witch, well she had, the
kindest blue eyes.
"That song that you sing,"
the girl then, did ask,
"What name do you call it? I
think that perchance,

It sounds as though if it's
one that I've known,
From far, far away. A place or a home."
The witch did reply, "You know of the tune?
The song, it belongs to the
Late Autumn Moon.

Few know of this song. Some
say it's from elves.
A magical tune. The lyrics compel."

The old witch then smiled. She reached in her bag.
The tattered old sack. A weathered torn rag.
She pulled out her hand and opened it up.
The thing that she held, could fit in a cup.

"I gather these things. These things that I've found.
They fall from these trees down onto the ground.
They're gifts from the woods. A secret you see?
My name is Anna. These are my trees.

These trees, well they offer their fine gifts to me,
And year after year, I take thankfully.
Look closely my dear. What is it I hold?
A ball? A round sphere? It's round and it's cold.

Do not be afraid. Remove all your fear.
My dreams have foretold. My song led you here.
Now listen to me. To learn and to know,
The magic surrounding these things that do grow."

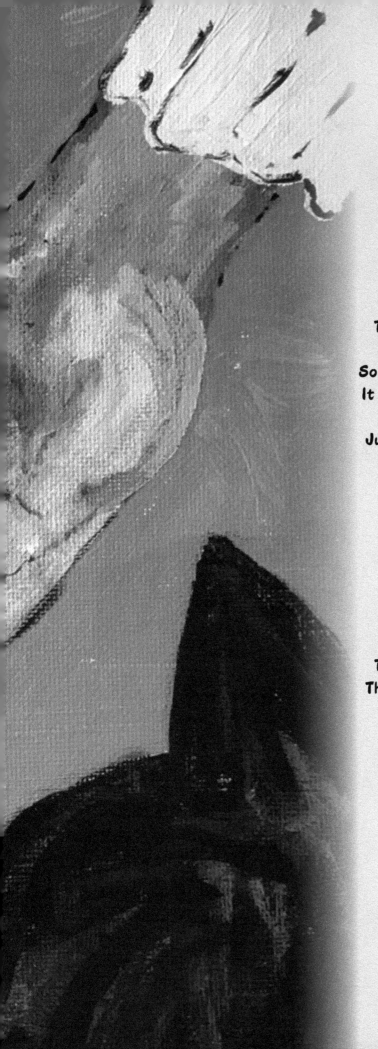

The old lady offered the brittle round ball.
The girl slowly took it in hands, oh small.
So plain and so ugly. 'Twas nothing quite grand.
It looked very simple. Still covered with sand.

Just where is the magic? Oh how could it be?
A spell dwelt inside it? This
homely large seed?
And then the witch snatched it.
She plucked it right back.
She placed the round ball
right back in her sack.

"It's time. Come with me.
We've more things to do.
The moon it sits low. The sky is light blue."
The girl stood up slowly. Now curious to see.
Where would the witch take
her? A new mystery.

They walked down a path that
lead through the woods,
In hushed quiet steps, as
soft as they could.
Then nearing the end, the girl finally saw,
A house dark and still, of
stone and old straw.

They walked to the back,
towards dark stony stairs.
Beneath the old house hid
a dank musty lair.
The girl, eyes wide open, heart
pounding could see,
This eerie cold place held hushed trickery.

Then something quite strange at once did occur;
The witch sang the tune quite clearly to her.
The moon in the sky, its powers awoke.
The magic revealed what shadows evoked.

A change to the place, from darkness to light.
The walls once in black, grew airy and bright.

They opened the door, still singing the tune,
And entered a whimsical warm fragrant room.
The images shifted, they ebbed and they flowed.
All so familiar. This place, how it glowed.

And as the room changed, the witch, she did too.
They transformed together. Ah ha! Deja vu?
The girl felt a presence. A time and a place.
It seemed so familiar. The room and her face.

But where had she seen them? Where, who, how and when?
She'd been here before. So when had it been?
And then she saw clearly. It was in a dream!
A dream she spent drifting upon a moonbeam.

The girl now looked fondly
upon the old shrew.
No longer in fear. Her heart, now it grew.
She smiled as she tilted her head lovingly.
The witch was a friend. She
plainly could see.

Then Anna stopped singing,
returning the smile,
"Sit down and be comfy.
We'll be here a while."
Onto a wood table she
placed the large sack
That carried round things
upon her old back.

Into the old sac, her hand it did go.
In search of just one. It moved to and fro.
She pulled out a ball with
both of her hands,
And spoke to the girl,
"Watch magic expand.

I gathered these up. Picked
up from the ground.
What came from the trees, they're
green and they're round.
Many might thing, a fruit or pear?
A lime or green apple? To
what they compare.

The walnut inside, its charms do attune.
But only when gathered
beneath the Fall Moon.
To you I do tell, for hence you were born,
To learn this from me. This
magic, I'm sworn."

They shelled all the nuts. They
picked and the poked.
They placed them in bowls of ancient old oak.
The black walnut scent, a smell oh so sweet.
Soon nuts would become a tasty new treat.

The witch worked and sang
the haunting old song,
Teaching the girl, as she sang along.
Together they weaved a spell in the air.
It drifted and lingered like
some ancient prayer.

Then into the bowl, they added more stuff.
The witch smiled and winked,
"This isn't enough.
We'll add some fresh eggs,
Some salt and then stir.
Brown sugar, some flour, some
butter, then churn.

Now let's see what's missing. Some maple?
Oh well. Instead some vanilla
completes this nice spell."
They stirred it all up. A sweet simple dough.
Then turned on the oven for baking just so.

They scooped out small lumps
to place on tin sheets.
In neat little rows for cookies so sweet.
Into the hot oven, the cookies they went,
To bake until crisp with rich golden scent.

The cookies, when done, smelled
better than great.
The girl somehow felt, she hardly could wait.
To taste one would be AMAZING! A treat!
A bite was so tempting. She wanted to eat.

These treats are
for you
The cookies
are sweet
So eat if
you're
blue.

They wrapped them up
tight, in little brown bags,
Tied up with a string with
notes on their tags.
The notes read the words,
"These treats are for you.
The cookies are sweet,
so eat if you're blue."

The old woman smiled
and said to the girl,
"It's time to now go.
To see all unfurl."
They gathered their
treats, each tiny small bag,
And walked out the door,
the girl and the hag.

They walked to the park.
The morning was late,
Now close to high noon.
The hour awaits.
"Our timing is good,"
the old lady said,
"It's time to now give and
share our shortbread."

Let's hand out our treats
to those that we see,
Are sad or just lonely,
who need company."
The girl looked around,
the park and the lake,
Then started to feel
a doubt, a mistake.

"No wait, I can't do this. I
don't know their names.
They don't even know me. They
might just complain."
"Now do not have fear,"
insisted the shrew.
"You'll find it's o.k. as long as you're true.

Let's hand out our gifts. They'll
try them, you'll see.
Now start with just one.
That boy by the tree."
The little boy sat alone by the tree.
His face was so sad. So what could it be?

"Hello there. Good day,"
the girl said to him.
"Why are you so sad? Why
are you so grim?"
"I've lost my new coin," he
said back to her.
"It's shiny and bright, but lost in the dirt."

She offered a bag, tied up with a string
And tagged with the note.
What good would this bring?
"Here take this. Who knows?
Perhaps this will do.
These cookies are great.
They're made just for you.

He opened the bag and took a big bite.
The cookie, it brought huge waves of delight.
Then just as he smiled, the magic drew near.
His coin glowed so bright as
the sun did appear.

He picked up the coin and held it up high,
Then rubbed off the dirt and let out a sigh.
He thanked her with joy, no longer so blue.
The girl felt so glad. The magic was true!

The witch winked at her and said with a smile,
"See that? How it works?
We'll be here a while."
"What's next," said the girl,
now ready for more,
"I see someone sad. See there at the shore?"

A woman alone, just by the lake's edge.
Her shoulders they shook. She sat on the ledge.
"Hello, can I help?" the little girl said.
"I'm sorry you're sad," she tilted her head.
"My grandmother's gone," the woman replied.
Her eyes were so sad. She looked up and sighed.
The girl took a bag and opened with haste.
A cookie might do, "Take one, have a taste."
The woman accepted and then had a bite.
A smile on her face began to grow bright.
"These taste like the cookies my grandmother baked."
The woman then smiled, although her heart ached.
"But this makes me happy.
This cookie tells me, it's here in my heart, she always will be."
They said their goodbyes and went on their way.
"What's next?" the girl said. "Let's help more today."
They walked in the park, together as one.
The witch and the girl, more work to be done.
They then saw a man, so sad and alone.
The witch knew him well, for often he roamed.

They found him quite cold,
alone on a bench.
Eyes down to the ground,
his hands he did clench.
His hair was snow white. His
clothes messed and torn.
No shoes on his feet. His
socks old and worn.

They went to the man with
tears in his eyes.
The sadness it showed.
He wanted to cry.
Then Anna said "Hi," and
held out her hand.
A cookie within, "Please
take a bite Sam."

He picked up the treat
and then took a bite.
A smile on his face showed
happy delight.
"Oh thank you. Where am I?
I walked through the frost.
I can't find my keys. I think I am lost.

I cannot remember my
house. Where is it?
I just don't recall. Not one little bit."
Then Anna just smiled, "Let's
bring you home Sam.
It's time to go back.
I know where I am.

We'll bring you home safe.
It's happened before.
Let's get you some shoes.
Your feet must be sore."

The four strolled along the
road and they talked.
The trees on the lane
swayed as they walked.

"We're here Sam. We're back.
We've brought you back home.
Please call me in need. You're never alone."
They said their farewells to
old Sam their friend.
Now sure he was safe, back
home in his bed.

The girl and the witch, now
done with their day,
Decided to go their own separate ways.
"I'll see you tomorrow," the
girl laughed and grinned,
"Let's do this again! Let's make
some more friends."

Before the witch answered,
the girl felt a chill.
The wind then stopped blowing.
The trees now stood still.
Her head felt so heavy, her
eyelids then closed.
The world spun around her.
It shifted, transposed.

She opened her eyes, now back in her bed.
Her covers were snuggled up close to her head.
And as she woke up, she waited to hear,
The old lady's song, but it was not there.

She turned and she listened. Where was the sweet song?
Where was the old lady? She waited so long.

She finally got up, and raced down the stairs.
She rushed out the door, through frigid cold air.
The wind whipped her face, her feet how they hurt.
The ground was so cold with frozen wet dirt.

And then the girl saw the
witch by the trees.
Anna was there, crouched
down on her knees.
The sun rose behind her.
She glowed in the dawn.
A smile caught her face as
she ran 'cross the lawn.

"Hello it is me!" the young girl did say.
"I waited to hear the
moon's song for today.
Why didn't you sing it?
I'm ready for more.
Please teach me more spells
and old ancient lore."

The witch gazed at her, so proud, it was clear.
The girl understood. Now ready to hear.
"I'm glad that you found me, for if you did not,
Then all that you learned would be lost. Forgot.

The moon has a tune, it's sweet and it's clear.
Just open your heart and then you will hear.
Now hum right along, as I sing the words.
We'll waken the fairies that fly with the birds."

The wind it swirled 'round them. It lifted up leaves.
The girl said to Anna, "I truly believe!"
"Believe in just what?" Anna asked as she glowed.
"In magic, in spells? Perhaps you should know.

You truly are something. So special I see.
So eager to learn of magic and glee.
But now I must tell you, for different we're not.
The magic we have, well, everyone's got.

No matter how big, no matter how small,
The magic you seek is part of us all.
There's something inside us. It's bright and it's true.
Believe that it's there, then joy will come through.

So here is the secret. It's time that I tell.
Through kindness and giving, the magic does dwell."

Magic Black Walnut Cookies

Ingredients
1 cup light brown sugar
1/2 cup butter
1 large egg
1 and 2/3 cups all-purpose flour
1/2 teaspoon baking soda
1/2 teaspoon salt
1 teaspoon vanilla
1 cup of chopped black walnuts
1 cup granulated sugar (for dipping)

Directions
Heat oven to 375 degrees
Grease a large baking sheet
Cream together in mixing bowl brown sugar and butter
Add egg and vanilla and beat well
Combine dry ingredients into another bowl
Combine dry and wet ingredients together
Add chopped black walnuts
Shape dough into small balls (about the size of walnuts)
Dip the cookie balls in sugar, place on baking sheet
Press with bottom of a glass to flatten slightly
Bake in the preheated oven for 12 to 15 minutes

Let cool, then place in small bags tied up with a string.
Give generously! The magic's within.

CPSIA information can be obtained
at www.ICGtesting.com
Printed in the USA
BVHW061346020620
580743BV00015B/171